NELLY MAY
Has Her Say

Cynthia DeFelice   Pictures by Henry Cole

Margaret Ferguson Books / Farrar Straus Giroux / New York

Farrar Straus Giroux Books for Young Readers
175 Fifth Avenue, New York 10010

Text copyright © 2013 by Cynthia DeFelice
Pictures copyright © 2013 by Henry Cole
Color separations by KHL Chroma Graphics Pte Ltd.
Printed in China by Toppan Leefung Printing Ltd.,
Dongguan City, Guangdong Province
Designed by Jay Colvin
First edition, 2013
1   3   5   7   9   10   8   6   4   2

mackids.com

Library of Congress Cataloging-in-Publication Data
DeFelice, Cynthia C.
    Nelly May has her say / Cynthia DeFelice ; pictures by Henry Cole. — 1st ed.
        p.   cm.
    Summary: A retelling of an old tale in which a servant girl's new master insists
she use uncommon names for common objects.
    ISBN 978-0-374-39899-6
    [1. Folklore—England.]   I. Cole, Henry, 1955–   ill.   II. Title.

PZ8.1.D3784Nel 2013
398.20942—dc23
                                                                                    2011018484

To Emi Olive, who has a lot to say!
—C.D.

To my dear friend Deb Greenwall, with love
—H.C.

Nelly May Nimble lived in a tiny cottage in the Bottoms with her parents, six younger brothers, and six younger sisters. There was never enough food to feed so many hungry mouths.

"I am old enough to earn my board and keep," Nelly May told her parents. "And I have heard that Lord Ignasius Pinkwinkle needs a new housekeeper and cook."

So the next morning Nelly May packed a bag with her few belongings, climbed the steep hill to the home of Lord Ignasius Pinkwinkle, and knocked on his door.

"I thought you might wish to hire me," said Nelly May. "I'm a grand cook, and neat as a pin."

"If you work for me," said Lord Pinkwinkle, "there are a few things you're going to have to learn."

"I'm good at learning things, sir," Nelly May assured him.

"Come inside then. I have special names for things, and I expect you to use them whenever you speak to me."

"Certainly, sir," said Nelly May.

"First and foremost, you are not to call me 'sir.' You are to address me as *Most Excellent of All Masters.*"

"*Most Excellent of All Masters,*" repeated Nelly May. "That's a fancy title, to be sure."

"Be certain to use it," said Lord Pinkwinkle. "Now let us tour the premises. We'll begin upstairs."

"Here, in my chamber, what is this?"

"That's simple," said Nelly May proudly. "It's your bed, which I expect I'll be making up for you."

"Not at all," said Lord Pinkwinkle. "That is not a bed. It is my restful slumberific."

"Your restful slumberific?" asked Nelly May doubtfully. "I never heard of such as that."

"Well, now you have," said Lord Pinkwinkle.

"Next, tell me, what do you see here?"

"Why," said Nelly May, "I see your dirty trousers, which I suppose I'll be washing and pressing."

"No, no, no! These are my long-legged limberjohns."

"Long-legged limberjohns, are they?" said Nelly May. "My, my, you could have fooled me."

"And these?" asked Lord Pinkwinkle.

"Those are your boots, if I may say so."

"You may not. And these are not boots, they are my stompinwhackers."

"Stompinwhackers, indeed," murmured Nelly May.

"Now to the parlor," said Lord Pinkwinkle. "What, pray tell, have we here?"

"A fire burning in the fireplace?" Nelly May asked hopefully.

"Of course not! It is a flaming pop-and-sizzle."

"A flaming pop-and-sizzle . . . Whatever was *I* thinking?" said Nelly May.

"And what is this creature that has been following us around?"

"That's nothing but a mangy old hound dog."

"Certainly not! He is my fur-faced fluffenbarker."

Nelly May sighed. "Your fur-faced fluffenbarker. Why didn't I guess that?"

"Oh, and this thing on the end of the fur-faced fluffenbarker, that
goes back and forth, and back and forth?"

"For mercy's sake, it's his tail."

"Not at all. It's his wigger-wagger."

"His wigger-wagger. If you say so . . ."

"I do," said Lord Pinkwinkle.

"Next is the kitchen. Do you know what this is?"

"Well, most folks would call it a bucket, or maybe a pail," ventured Nelly May. "But there's no telling what you'll be calling it."

"I call it a wet scooperooty, and so must you."

"If I must," said Nelly May.

"And inside? What is this?"

"Criminy! Look what you've done! You've poured water all over the floor!"

"It's not water but rivertrickle, silly girl."

"It needs mopping up, no matter what you call it," grumbled Nelly May.

"You can do that in a moment. Now, let's go outside, shall we?"

"Tell me, what is the name for this entire magnificent edifice?"

"*I* would call it your house . . . but I'll lay odds that's not the right answer," muttered Nelly May.

"Indeed it is not. This is my roof-topped castleorum."

"Roof-topped castleorum. Whatever you say."

"I say it's high time for you to get to work. But let us not forget my special name for *you*."

"For *me*? Why, I thought I was to be the housekeeper and cook."

"No, no, that will never do. From here on, you will be my fuzzy-dust-and-fooder."

To that, all Nelly May could say was, "Hmmph."

That afternoon, as she
mopped the floor,

cleaned the stairs,

and cooked supper, Nelly May wondered what she had gotten herself
into. But she was a good, smart girl, and she needed a job. So she
practiced Lord Pinkwinkle's special names over and over until she knew
them by heart.

And it's a good thing she did, because that very night she was awakened from a sound sleep. She sniffed the air, then leaped from her bed and ran to the parlor, where something was terribly wrong!

She dashed up the stairs to Lord Pinkwinkle's chamber, banged on the door, and shouted, "Most Excellent of All Masters! Get out of your restful slumberific and put on your long-legged limberjohns and your stompinwhackers. A spark of flaming pop-and-sizzle got on the fur-faced fluffenbarker's wigger-wagger, and if you don't get a wet scooperooty full of rivertrickle quickly, you'll lose your roof-topped castleorum and everything in it! And one more thing, Most Excellent of All Masters, get yourself a new fuzzy-dust-and-fooder, because I quit!"

Nelly May went out the door, down the hill, and back to the Bottoms, where she curled up in bed with her six little sisters.

The next morning, to her great surprise, who should come knocking
at the door but Lord Ignasius Pinkwinkle himself.

"Good day to you, Miss Nelly May," he said. "You saved my house and my dog and I thank you from the bottom of my heart. What's more, I like you. You're clever and quick. Might you be willing to return as my housekeeper and cook?"

"I might," said Nelly May. "But if I do, must I use your special names?"

"Just one," said Lord Pinkwinkle.

"And what name is that?" asked Nelly May.

"Well, my dear old nursey used to call me Pinky . . ." Lord Pinkwinkle said.

Nelly May smiled. "It would be my pleasure to work for you, Pinky."